Sharon's Family

Sharon was sitting at the breakfast table alone, cum slowly dripping from her mouth down on her naked tits. She'd just finished sucking off her two sons before they went to their summer job, her husband left before breakfast.

She was thinking back when it had all started, it was almost four years ago now. They were living in a nice neighbourhood, both had good jobs and they had two wonderful children, two sons. In their earlier days of marriage they had a wonderful sex life, both very interested in experimenting with sex, they had participated in group sex, they both loved cumplays and other more perverse games. When the kids came, the sex life became more subdued, but they still managed to enjoy each other frequently.

She came home from work one day a little earlier than normal and when she entered the house, she heard moaning from upstairs. Immediately she thought something has happened to one of her children, but when she reached the top of the stairs, the moaning was not because someone was in pain, quite the opposite.

The door to her eldest son's room, age 19, was ajar and she sneaked up and almost gasped at the sight. Rob was lying on his bed, a magazine in one hand and with other stroking his hard cock. She had never seen his cock erect, although she had caught glimpses of it when he walked down the corridor naked on his way to the bathroom. It was a beautiful cock, 8 " long and quite thick, but what impressed her most was his balls, they were very large and looking like they could burst. She felt ashamed looking at her son like this, but at the same time she couldn't take her eyes away from the beautiful sight. Rob started to move his hand faster now, his stomach muscles started to flex, he let go of the magazine and with a grunt he came in huge spurts over himself, some of them almost reaching his chest. It looked incredible sexy and Sharon could feel herself getting wet. She turned around and went downstairs, where she hurried to the bathroom, locked the door and rubbed herself to an orgasm, which nearly took her breath away.

While she was recovering, she again felt ashamed, but the sight of her eldest sons hard cock and the cum spurting from it, really turned her on. She remembered in past times, when she and her husband had played games, she had enjoyed teasing him for hours and then see how far he could shoot, her open mouth always ready to receive his cum.

During the dinner that night, she could hardly keep her eyes from her Rob, thinking how he had turned her on, imagining his hard cock.

The next several weeks she tried to get off work earlier and she caught her son jerking off more than once, always enjoying the sight of his spurting cock. Then one day, as she was getting out of the shower, she was greeted by Rob, sitting naked on the toilet, playing with his cock.

"Oh my god," she said, "what are you doing, Get out of here at once."

"I don't think so, "he said smiling," you have enjoyed me so many times looking through my door, now it's my turn to have some fun."

"What are you talking about," she stammered.

"Don't you think I've seen you watching me, the look in your eyes when I cum"

She stood there naked looking at her son playing with his now hard cock.

"What are you going to do," she asked

"Not much, you have to do all the work. I want you to give me a hand job," Rob said.

"Oh no, I couldn't do that, it's both illegal and also immoral."

"Well, how would you like others to find out you're spying on your son while he jerks off", he asked.

"Please, don't tell" she pleaded, "I'll do it."

She fell to her knees and started to fondle his cock. It was soon throbbing in her hand and she started to jerk him off, moving her hand slowly up and down the shaft. After a while Rob started to squirm on the toilet, Sharon picked up the speed and soon he gasped.

"Oh my god, I'm going to cum, this is so good," he panted.

"Yes, cum for mommy, let me see your hot cum," she moaned.

"Oh yes, I'm cumming"

She looked at the purple head of his cock and soon the hot sperm was shooting out from his cock. The first two spurts covered her hands and then she pushed the cock down, so the rest landed on her big tits. He looked in amazement at his mom between his legs, looking lovingly at his cock while it spurted hot cum over her tits.

Sharon milked the last cum from his cock and the started to rub the milky fluid into her skin. She lifted her hand and tasted his cum, looking at him while she did it.

He stared unbelievingly at this; it was beyond his wildest dream, his hot, sexy mom licking his cum from her fingers after having jerked him off.

"This will be our secret," she told Rob, "if you don't tell, maybe we can do it again."

"Don't worry, I won't tell anyone."

After this it became a regular thing, she would come home from work and he would be waiting in his room, lying naked with a hard-on, waiting for her. Sometimes she would jerk him off, making him cum all over her tits, at other times she would suck his cock, taking it all in her mouth when he came.

This worked for a while, but eventually she was caught by her husband, when she emerged from Rob's room with her tits all covered in cum.

Phil couldn't believe his own eyes, when he saw Sharon coming from Rob's room, tits hanging out and glistering with cum.

"What the hell is going on here," he asked an almost paralysed Sharon.

"Ahh, well, it's not like you think," she stammered.

"Well, it certainly looks like cum on you tits and coming from our son's room, it does not take a genius to figure out what's happened."

She just stood there with cum dripping from her tits, didn't know what to say.

Then he did something unexpected. He went to her, kissed her on the mouth and started fondling her tits.

"I hope you enjoyed it, it looks like he's cum a lot," he asked her.

Sharon just looked at her husband, couldn't believe what was happening.

"Yes, he came a lot, just like you used to do. He has a wonderful cock."

Phil took her by the arm, led her to the bedroom and undressed. He almost threw her on the bed and spread her legs, then rammed his now throbbing cock in her pussy. They fucked hard, she managed to cum twice before he came in her pussy.

After they had caught their breath, he said:

"I don't mind you fucking and sucking Rob, but I think it's not fair to Peter, he should have the same opportunity to get laid, after all he's only one year younger than Rob."

She just looked at him, could not believe her own ears. She stroked his wet cock:

"Oh, I would love to do that. Makes me all wet again, thinking about all the cocks I can enjoy now."

After a few days, she had managed to seduce the youngest son as well, catching him in the shower.

"Hey mom, what about a little privacy here," Peter had shouted when she entered the bathroom.

"Don't worry, son, I've seen naked men before."

She had started to undress and it had the desired effect. She could see Peter's cock starting to get hard.

"What are you doing, I'm trying to take a shower."

"Yeah, well you better hurry then, I'm next," Sharon said, now naked and fondling her tits.

Peter could not help himself, his cock was now rock hard, and seeing his mom naked was a dream cum true. He'd often stolen a glimpse of her when she changed her clothes, jerking off like a mad afterwards.

He turned off the shower and stepped out.

"Could you please hand me a towel," he asked his mum.

"Yeah, sure, but why don't I dry you off," Sharon asked.

She took a towel from the rack and started to dry his body. He was a quarterback on the local football team and had a great body. When the back was done, she started on the front, noticing with delight Peter's cock was even bigger than Rob's, not much but still enough to notice.

She rubbed his body with the towel and soon reached his cock.

"Ah mom, I think I better do that myself," he said, blushing.

"No, that's all right, I don't mind. It this because of me," she asked teasingly.

"Well yes, I think you have a beautiful body."

"Nice of you to say so, would you like me to help you a little?"

"Please, yes mom," Peter panted.

Sharon took hold of Peter's cock and started rubbing it. She got down to her knees and kissed the forehead of his cock.

"Would you like me to suck your cock?" she asked.

"Oh yes, please suck my cock, mom," he gasped.

"Looks like you haven't cum for a few days, is that so?"

"You know the coach have told us not to jerk off the week before a game," Peter said.

"What an evil man. Well, I'm gonna change that right now."

She took the head of his cock in her mouth and jerked on the shaft with both hands. She started sucking and soon she could feel his legs tremble.

"Are you going to cum soon," she asked.

"Oh yes, but mom, I've been drank a lot of beers last night and I always cum so much after drinking beers."

"That's ok Peter, just give it all to me."

He looked down at his mom; she had his cock in her mouth and was looking up at him. He let out a groan and started to erupt in her mouth.

Sharon felt the first blast hit the back of her mouth and soon her mouth was full of cum, it started to run from the sides of her moth as well, while Peter was pushing his cock into her mouth. After several spurts, she let go of his cock, looked up at him, showing him all his cum in her mouth, she played with her tongue and then swallowed it all. Peter looked with staring eyes down at his mom, his cock now half erect and still dripping cum.

Sharon got up and kissed Peter. At first he was shocked, but the started to kiss her as well, tasting his own cum.

After that day, she fucked and sucked the male members of the family as often as they liked, now it was easier, all knew and they took advantage of her in every situation. When they had dinner, she was often under the table sucking cocks, while the men ate. After dinner they would retreat to the living room, where she rode and sucked their cocks, while they watched TV.

The sons would often fuck her before Phil came home, so more than once he had arrived home just to find her hurrying down the stairs with cum on her face or dripping from her pussy, ready to serve her husband.

When they had the time in the weekends, the sex was more advanced. The men saved their cum for a few days and then they would use her for hours, with a cumbath as the reward.

Would you like to hear more, maybe some of the boy's friends could come along, femdom girlfriends...

After having started sucking off her two sons, she and Phil's sex life became a lot better. He always got much exited, when thinking of her servicing the sons and they fucked much more than they used to.

He would come home to find her just finished with her duties, sometimes he would have to wait for her finishing sucking off her sons. Then they would retreat to the master bedroom and while he was fucking her, she would tell him all the details.

One day he found them all together, a thing which has not happened before. Although both the boys they knew what was going on, she'd never done them both at the same time. She was on her knees in front of them, naked to the waist and stroking their cocks.

"Come on, spurt for me, I want to taste all your cum," she told the boys.

They stood beside each other grinning, this was great, their mother on her knees with her big tits naked, waiting for them to give their loads.

"Rob, you want to come first?" Peter asked, while he was breathing hard.

"We can come together" Rob replied," see if she can take all of our cum."

"Oh yes" Sharon still stroking the boys hard cocks," do it for me, come in my mouth."

She looked up at the smiling boys, their cocks throbbing in her hands. A little pre-cum was forming at the head of Peter's cock, she teasingly licked it off. His cock gave a jolt and she could feel he was close to coming. She intensified the stroking of Rob's cock, so they could come together.

"Oh mum, I'm coming," Peter gasped.

"Yeah, me too, watch out mum, here it comes" Rob said.

Phil was standing in the door to the kitchen and he watched in amazement the scenario in front of him. There was his beautiful wife, dressed in a miniskirt with her top pulled down to her waist, her big tits naked, in front of his sons, urging them to come in her mouth.

Moments later she felt the first spurt of hot cum hitting her chin and soon both boys was shooting their loads on her face, aiming for her mouth. They were quite good at it, most of the cum landed between her lips, a few spurts plastered her chin and nose.

She let go of their cocks and licked her lips, showing them the cum in her mouth where she played with it with her tongue. She then closed her lips and swallowed.

"Uh, so much. Have you been thinking about me the whole day?" she asked her voice thick with cum.

"Yes, I certainly have. I really was looking forward to getting a blowjob when I came home."

"Yeah, me too," Rob said," I almost had to jerk off in my lunch break, I was so horny."

"Well done boys," Phil said," you know what your mother likes."

They spun around and looked at Phil, standing in the kitchen door, stroking his hard cock.

"Why don't you come over here and continue, Sharon?" he asked.

She smiled at him and got up, her big tits swaying as she walked to the kitchen door. He could see small strands of cum on her tits; she hadn't been able to swallow it all.

"Have you saved your cum for as well?" she asked, grabbing his cock.

"Yes, travelling for a week without jerking off should do the trick."

The boys watched with still hard cocks as their mother knelt before her husband, stroking his cock and began sucking him off. Her mouth slowly engulfed the head and she started to suck, moving her head back and forth, playing along the hardness with her tongue, teasing him with the tip at the forehead.

"Damn, you're good at this. Don't you agree, boys? Your mom is a great cocksucker."

"Yeah dad, she's really good. She likes it when we cum in her mouth."

"Well then, why don't you join me, looks like you're ready again."

The boys quickly moved in position, so their mother was surrounded by three cocks. She let go of Phil's cock and looked around, licked her lips and said:

"What a sight, are all these nice cocks for me?"

"Yes," Phil said," they are all for you and now it's all a bit more in the open, you'll service us whenever we need to."

"But Phil, that sounds like I'm a horrible slut?"

"Well, exactly, you're our slut now and you'll do whatever we tell you to do. So now get on with sucking."

She looked up at him, smiled and took his hard cock in her mouth again, while she was stroking the boys. She took turns sucking them off even though the boys had come in her mouth earlier, it didn't take long before all cocks were ready to burst again.

"Are you ready boys?" Phil panted," I'm just about to cum?"

"Yeah dad, go ahead, give her all you got."

"Ok, here it comes," he said, directing his cock towards Sharon's face.

Moments later his cock twisted and the first spurt hit her in the face, covering her nose and chin. The next she managed to catch with her mouth, but some of it also escaped her mouth, dripping down her chin to her big tits.

The boys watched with admiration, they had never seen so much cum before; only maybe on the DVD's they sometimes rented. Their father had been gone for a week and it showed. When he was finished, Sharon's face was drenched in cum, it was dripping from her nose and chin and her tongue was covered in sperm.

She looked up at Phil and the boys with glowing eyes, licking her lips, so they could all see the cum in her mouth, opening her mouth, waiting for more.

"My god, look at her, she really loves cum. Are you guys ready to give her some more?" Phil asked.

Without answering, both the boys started to erupt over their mother, shooting their hot juices all over her. She managed to catch some of it with her mouth, but a lot landed on her face, covering her nose and chins. When they were done, she looked a mess, with cum all over her face, some in her hair and dripping from her lips.

The three men stood exhausted and looked at Sharon; she then started to get up and went to the kitchen table, reaching for the tissues.

"No, don't wipe it off," Phil said, "I like the way you look now, all covered in our cum. Leave it as it is."

"But it will ruin my dress, if I don't clean up."

"Well then, don't put it on. Actually from now on, don't wear any top when we're around. What about that, boys, wouldn't you like to see your mother topless around the house when we're home?"

"Yeah dad" they both said," that would be cool, having mom walking around with her tits naked all the time. What did you mean precisely by her being our slut?"

"She's obviously getting really into this, so I think she should be available to us all the time, doing whatever we want her to. Later I will tell you some stories about what we did before you were around, that might help you to understand what a slut she can be."

Sharon smiled at the memories of what they had been doing in the younger years. She turned around, facing the men, sperm still covering her tits.

"Ok, but I must warn you, I need a lot of cock when I first get going, do you think you can handle that?"

"Sure we can, can't we dad?" both Rob and Peter replied.

"You just wait sweetheart, you'll get all the cock you want."

Sharon was slowly transformed from a loving, decent housewife to a slut; her main task was to service the men in her life.

She was in her late 40's, still a very attractive woman, medium height and with natural blonde hair. She had nice legs and a firm ass, but her most sexy feature was her tits. They were big and still firm, with nature just beginning do its thing, slightly sagging, but it made the appearance so much sexier, a real mature woman to look at.

These tits were now on display for the guys in the house and it worked, they were all in a constant state of arousal.

When she was serving breakfast, she would stroll around in the kitchen, tits swaying and the boys could not keep their eyes of her. They kept stroking their cocks in their shorts and it often ended with her sucking them off before they left home in the morning.

When it was weekend, the sex became more intense. That had started a week or so after she had sucked them all off. It was Friday evening; Phil sat on the patio and drank a few beers with his sons and Sharon did some housework, but she would also make frequent trips to the men to make sure they didn't run out of beer.

"Hey Sharon, how about a little entertainment?" Phil said.

"What did you have in mind," Sharon asked.

"Why don't you put on some of the lingerie I've bought for you, then you can do a little striptease for us," he answered.

"Ok, that could be fun, but we might have to go inside."

"No, that's alright, I don't think the neighbours can see us here."

She smiled at him at went into the house. A few minutes later she was back, dressed in high heels, black stockings and a black transparent negligee. She slowly danced around on the patio, teasing the men by groping their crotches and revealing her body. She started to take her top off and both Phil and the boys were having difficulties concealing their hard cocks.

"Why don't you all show me your cocks, are they nice and hard?"

They all dropped their pants quickly and now she could see the effect she had on them, the cocks were very hard and throbbing. She was now naked apart from her high heels and stockings; still she was flirting with the men, fondling their cocks when she passed them.

"Come over here" Phil ordered," I want to feel if you're wet."

She stepped up to her husband and he started to feel her up, she was dripping with juices. He spun her around and forced her down on his cock. She let out a moan as his big cock slipped into her warm pussy. The boys started to jerk of at the sight of the mother riding on their father's big cock.

"Hey boys, don't be shy, come over here and let me see you jerk off," Sharon said.

Both jumped out of their chairs and stood in front of their mother, slowly stroking their cocks.

She was still riding Phil and at the same time caressing her big tits, offering them to the boys. Soon Phil was starting to jerk in his seat and he came with a moan, filling his wife's pussy with cum. She also reached her climax, grinding her pussy on his cock and moaning loudly.

When she calmed down, she got up, cum dripping from her pussy, and grabbed both the boys by their cocks.

"Come on; let's go inside, I need more cock."

They followed their mother inside, where she laid down on the sofa, spread her pussy-lips, inserting two fingers and massaging her tits with the other hand.

"Uh, fuck me now, I need to be fucked by both of you" she gasped, "Rob, you do it first, I can suck Peter at the same time."

Rob quickly entered her; with one thrust he slipped the whole length of his hard cock in her wet pussy, while Peter lowered his hard cock to her mouth. She greedily started sucking on it, jerking it with one hand and using her mouth and lips.

Peter stared down at his mother, what a sight. She was sucking at his cock; his brother was fucking her, her big tits moving back and forth as Rob slammed his cock into her pussy.

"Mom, can I fuck your tits?" Peter asked.

"Yes, of course" she said, letting go of his cock and pushing her tits together, "put your big cock between my tits".

Peter slipped his cock between her tits and began fucking them, thrusting his cock in and out, and his cock-head sometimes hitting her jaw, where she could lick it.

Rob meanwhile started breathing heavily and moaning he was coming. He started to fuck his mother even faster, gripping her legs and pounding her wet pussy. He let out a groan and came in her, cum starting to escape from the side of his cock as he pushed it far up her pussy. At the same time Peter fucked her tits harder, while she gasped:

"Oh Peter, fuck my tits, I want to feel your cum, jerk of all over me," she moaned.

Peter could feel the pressure of his cum, he gave one final thrust and the hot sperm jetted from the tip of his cock, plastering his mother's face, the last spurts landed on her tits. She licked her lips, savouring the taste of the hot cum and massaged her tits, so they were glistering.

Phil had watched the scene with great pleasure; he was now sitting in a couch next to them, stroking his hard cock.

"Sharon, I'm ready to cum again, do you want more cum?"

"Yes, give it to me; I want to taste your hot cum."

Phil got up and stood in front of his wife, she was sitting in the sofa now, mouth open, ready to receive his cum.

"No, don't open your mouth, I want to cum all over your face, so we can have something sexy to look at while we eat," he said.

She obediently closed her mouth, looked up at him, begging for his cum. He moved closer to her and started to stroke his cock faster in front of her face. Soon he was erupting in huge spurts all over her face; it ended on her forehead, her nose and on her chin. She looked real messy when he was done, his fresh cum combined with the loads she had received before made her face look like it was glazed.

"Ok boys, that was good, you really can give a slut what she needs," Phil said.

"I'm hungry now, go make some food for us, Sharon," he ordered.

"But I need to freshen up and get dressed," she protested.

"No, just make the food and come and eat with us as you are, you have eaten before with cum on your face, remember in Key West?" Phil said.

She smiled at this, gave his cock a squeeze and went into the house, cum still on her face and dripping from her tits and pussy.

"What happened at Key West?" the boys asked.

"We were on vacation there and one day after while we were driving, your mother started to play with my cock. I parked and she wanted to suck me of, daring me to do it in the parking place. I accepted, but in return she had to promise to do what I said afterwards. I came all over her face and when I was done, we drove to a Pizzahut nearby. I made her order and made very sure she was visible to the young woman in the window, when she paid. Poor thing, she probably never seen anyone with cum all over face, paying for her meal. We then parked in a quite busy parking lot and ate our pizzas, your mother still on full display."

When he was done telling the story, Sharon called them dinner. They sat down at the table, while she served them their food. She was still only in her high heels and stocking, her face and tits were still wet with cum as she sat down to join them. They ate and talked, the men commented on her slutty looks, they all thought it looked extremely sexy she was still covered in cum.

"Well, I don't mind" she said, "it's quite exiting to sit here, dripping with cum and knowing there's plenty more where that came from."

From that day on, they were fucking more regularly. Often when the boys came home, they would find their mother either walking almost naked around the house or sitting in the living-room, waiting for them to arrive. She taught them to eat pussy; she would direct them while they were between her legs licking her shaved pussy, instructing them how best to give a woman pleasure. Mostly they were rewarded with blowjob or a nice long fuck, of if they were both home, she would blow one while the other fucked her, then change them around after they had cum.

Some months passed like this, then one day Rob proudly announced he had found a girlfriend.

"Oh Rob, I'm so happy for you, although I'm going to miss your cock, "Sharon said with a grin.

"Well done my son, when can we see her?" Phil asked.

"Actually, she coming over tonight, so I think its best mom puts on some clothes" Rob answered.

"Off course, otherwise the poor girl will be scared away," his mother remarked.

Later that day, Rob introduced them to Karen, a stunning blonde with an extremely sexy body. She was very well received by the family and they all got along quite well. After having had some good food and some drinks, it was time for Karen to get home. They suddenly realized they all had too much to drink, so she accepted the offer to stay for the night.

"Mom, is it ok if she sleeps in my room?" Rob asked.

"Well of course darling, if she needs anything just let me know," Sharon said.

A few moments later there was a knock on the door to the master bedroom, Phil opened it and saw Karen standing outside only in a loose shirt. It showed off her magnificent tanned legs, you could just see the outline of her firm tits.

"Sharon said if I needed anything, I could ask her," Karen said.

"Sure darling, what do you need?" Sharon asked from the bed.

"I need something to remove my makeup with" Karen said

"Come with me, I have some in our bathroom", she said and led Karen to the bathroom attached to the master bedroom.

Once in there, she gave Karen what she needed and stood back admiring her body.

"You certainly have a very nice body, Karen, do you work out much?"

"No, not really, I think I'm just blessed from nature's side. The only thing I would like to have is larger breasts, I think they are too small. Yours is much nicer, if you don't mind me saying so."

"Well thank you, no I don't mind. But yours are just perfect for your body. Off course I know most men like big tits, but you have such a wonderful body, so don't worry. You'll get you share of men" Sharon said.

The said goodnight and Karen went to Rob's room.

"Your mother is a very nice woman" she said, as she climbed into Rob's bed.

"Yes, she wonderful in many ways" Rob replied smiling.

After they made love, they both fell asleep, but an hour later Karen woke up to strange noises.

It came from the hallway and she couldn't resist taking a peek. She opened the door and tiptoed into the corridor. The noises came from the master bedroom, where the door was ajar and when she was close enough, she could actually see the bed and what she saw, made her stare wide-eyed.

Sharon was riding her husband and her son Peter was fucking her from behind. She had off course heard about double penetration before, but she had never seen it. And then with her son!

The threesome on the bed changed position; she was now blowing her son while her husband fucked her and moments later they both showered her with cum, as they came all over her face.

She quickly went back to Rob's room and slid into bed with him. She woke him up, all exited and very wet.

"Do you know what I just saw?" she asked him.

"No, but it must have been something nice, you're all dripping," Rob said, as he felt her wet pussy.

"I just saw your mom being fucked by your dad and your brother" she whispered.

"Oh no, they promised to behave while you are here," Rob moaned.

"Do you mean you know about this? Oh my god, have you been doing it yourselves?" she asked, breathing a little heavier.

"I guess there no way of covering this now, yes I've fucked my mom as well. Does that mean it's all over now?" he asked.

"No silly, I think it's very exiting. Your mother has a great body; I can understand your needs. What do you do to her, tell me, does she suck you off or do you fuck her?"

"It started with her sucking us off, but then dad found out and now she's our slut, she'll do anything we ask her to."

"Wow, you really mean anything. This is so exiting, come, fuck me again."

They fucked intensively for almost an hour, all the time he told her what he and the other men in the house had done his mother. Starting from the sucking off in the bathroom to the weekends full of sex, with Sharon being used a target for circle jerk, sucking them off during dinner and the cum-showers that normally followed a fucking session.

The next morning they all gathered at the breakfast table, all acting normal, Sharon serving the meal.

After they were finished, Karen looked at Rob and nodded.

Rob got up and stood beside his mother, whipped out his cock and said:

"Mom, I need you to suck my cock."

"But Rob, what are you doing, behave yourselves, what must Karen be thinking?" Sharon stammered.

"I think you should do it, Rob has told me all about it and I saw how you fucked your other son yesterday evening. So go ahead, I don't mind, I would like to see a real slut doing it," Karen said.

Phil lightened up; clearly this young girl was no prude.

"Go ahead, Sharon, show her what you can do."

Sharon reluctantly started to suck Rob's cock, which was soon very hard.

"Can you taste something different, he has been fucking me all night? So that's my juices you can taste on his cock," Karen teased.

This made Sharon suck even harder, realizing it was another woman's juices covering his cock. Phil helped her take off most of her clothes, so they could all enjoy her big tits. Karen was also undressing now; all eyes were drawn to her tanned, firm body.

"Rob, I need you to fuck me now", she said.

He obediently pulled his cock out of his mother's mouth and quickly moved over to Karen, where he started to fuck her.

Sharon found herself without cock, but not for long, as both the others soon was at her side, stroking their cocks. She started to suck them off, while she looked at her son fucking his girlfriend.

Both Peter and Phil were soon ready to come and when their loads landed on Sharon's face and tits, Karen let out a scream and came in a gigantic orgasm, while Rob erupted in her pussy.

Karen soon found her breath and looked at Sharon, her face and tits covered with cum.

"Sharon, you look like a real slut. I have some cum for you as well, lie down on the table," she ordered.

Sharon placed herself on the table on her back and Karen straddled the mature woman and looked down at her with lust in her eyes.

"This is so good; I've always wanted to dominate a mature slut."

"Now, if we're going to keep this a secret, you must also do what I want, understood?"

"Yes Karen, please tell me what you want," Sharon replied, looking up at the blonde goddess standing above her.

She squatted over Sharon's face and spread her pussy lips.

"Lick your son's cum from my pussy. And whenever I feel like it, you must lick me until I come."

Without waiting for an answer, she lowered her pussy to Sharon's lips and made her lick the sticky cum from it.

After Karen joined the family, Sharon's sexual services were even more in demand than before. She really liked the young woman and Karen was only happy to use her every way she could think of.

Sharon always had a submissive streak in her personality, but it was never explored in full before now. She was satisfied when someone took the decisions in her life, also of course in her sex life. When they were younger, Phil often dared her to try new things, things that she secretly dreamed of, but never told anyone about. He introduced her to oral and anal sex, they experimented with sex in public places and she learned to love the taste of cum.

Now with all the male members of her family using her at every opportunity, she was only delighted at the addition of a new member and Karen had her own ways of treating her.

Sharon stayed at their house most of time, so when her family came home, she was ready to serve them. Karen worked at a restaurant and had varied working hours, so she was often home during daytime.

"Sharon" Karen called out, "where are you?"

She had just entered the front door and was looking for her mother-in-law.

"Karen, what a nice surprise" Sharon answered, coming down from the first floor, "I was just getting ready for the boys."

She was dressed, as she knew the boys liked it, in high heels and black fishnet stockings, suspenders and nothing else. Her big tits swayed as she approached Karen, embracing her as they met, her tits pressed against the young girl.

Karen fondled her breasts and admired her body, she stilled looked very sexy for a mid-aged woman, her ass still firm and her legs in fantastic shape.

She let her hands explore further down and soon she was caressing the moist pussy, spreading the pussy lips and probing the pussy with a finger. Sharon was already very wet, anticipating an afternoon filled with sex when the boys came home.

"You have a very tight pussy, Sharon, but I think it would look better naked. Do you want me to shave you?" she asked.

"Oh yes, that would be nice. I normally only trim it, but being totally naked would be even better."

"Come on then, let's go upstairs" Karen said.

Sharon followed the young woman up the stairs, admiring her tanned legs and firm ass. It was summertime and she could see, Karen was wearing a G-string underneath her white shorts.

She started fantasizing of undressing the young woman and serving her in every way the she could think of. The thought made her shiver with lust.

When they entered the bathroom, Sharon sat on the edge of the bathtub and was ordered to spread her legs. Karen knelt between her legs and looked at the beautiful sight of Sharon's well-used pussy. First she used an electric shaver and when Sharon's pubic hair was as short as she could manage, she applied the shaving foam and started to use the razor blade. Sharon really enjoyed the feeling of her daughter-in-law using the shaver at her pussy and she could feel herself get wet.

A little while later Karen was all done and she spread Sharon's pussy-lips, looking at the juices flowing from her pussy all the way down to her ass.

"Wow, it really looks good when you're all naked. Seems it turns you on as well, you are all wet."

"Yes, it's the way you make me feel when you use the razor. My pussy gets so sensitive."

Karen moved closer and started to lick the moist pussy in front of her, spreading the lips and licking at her clit.

"Oh my god, please don't stop, it feels so good," Sharon moaned.

Karen licked the mature woman's pussy and soon Sharon came, bucking her hips up and down, covering the young woman's face with juices.

After she settled down, she knelt in front of Karen and kissed her face, tasting her own cunt-juices. She asked if she could return the favor.

Karen quickly dropped her clothes and straddled Sharon's face. She looked down at Sharon's exited face, spread her pussy lips and watched a small string of moisture dripping from her pussy. Quickly she moved her pussy over Sharon's mouth, letting it drip on her tongue.

Sharon moved her tongue in circles, catching the flow of juices. Karen lowered her pussy and started to move it back and forth over her mouth.

"Oh yes, lick my cunt, I'm going to cum all over your face, keep licking" Karen moaned.

"Mmm, you taste so good," Sharon said between licks" I never get tired of serving you."

"Well if you do a good job, maybe I'll let you lick my ass too," Karen answered.

"Yes, let me lick your beautiful ass, turn around."

Karen lifted her pussy, juices dripping all over her Sharon's face, and leaned forward, spreading her ass.

"Come on, lick my ass, I really love to feel your tongue back there."

Sharon started to move her tongue up and down the crack of Karen's ass, letting her tongue probe her hole.

"Oh yeah, stick your tongue in there," Karen gasped.

Sharon intensified her effort, pushing the tip of her tongue in the young woman's ass, moving her head back and forth and fucking her with it.

Soon Karen's ass was moving up and down, she pushed it into the older woman's face while she grabbed her hair.

"Holy shit," a voice said, "look at that. I didn't know she would do that."

Karen looked up and saw Rob standing in the door, stoking his cock. Just behind him were Peter and one of his friends. Peter's friend just looked openmouthed at the sight of Rob's girlfriend getting a rim job from their mother.

"Hey honey, come on over here, let me suck on that," Karen urged Rob.

He quickly went over to the two women and stuck his cock in Karen's mouth. She eagerly started sucking on the erect cock, while Sharon was still eating her ass.

Peter explained to his friend Chris that their mother was their slut and they could use her every way the wanted. Chris was obviously very exited at that idea and wanted to know if she would serve him as well.

"Well, drop your pants and come with me," Peter said and got rid of his own clothes.

They boys went over to the threesome and Peter asked Karen, if she was all done with Sharon. Karen took Peter's cock of out her mouth:

"Yeah, go ahead, she can always finish me off later. Now I need to be fucked."

Sharon reluctantly let go of Karen's ass and faced the two boys. She licked her lips at the sight of two erect cocks and started to fondle her tits.

"You both horny?" she teased them," well come on then, let me suck your cocks."

They both came closer and soon they were poking their cocks in her face. She grabbed hold of both of them and started to jerk them off. Chris was not used to this treatment, so without warning he came and plastered Sharon's face with his cum. She was taken by surprise by his early orgasm, but quickly opened her moth and directed the spurts between her lips.

When he was done, his cum was dripping from her nose and she stuck her tongue out, trying to catch it. She smiled at Chris, showing him the cum in her mouth:

"My my, you were really fast and so much cum. Well, it doesn't matter. You're a young man and can cum again soon, am I right?"

"Yes, I normally can cum two or three time a day. Will you suck my cock also?"

Without hesitation she took the still erect cock in her mouth, cum dripping from the sides of her mouth while she sucked his cock.

Peter grinned at the sight:

"See, I told you, she just loves to give head."

Chris just nodded; he was looking down at Sharon, still not believing the sight in front of him. There was his best friends mom sucking his cock, her big tits covered with his cum, which was dripping from her face and mouth. She was still stroking Peter's cock and now took turns sucking them both, urging them to cum in her mouth.

"Come on guys, which on of you can cum in my mouth first. I want to taste all you cum."

Rob was now fucking Karen from behind, his big cock thrusting in and out of her dripping pussy. Her ass was glistering from the licking Sharon had done, looking very inviting.

Rob withdraws from her pussy and pushed the tip of his cock at her ass.

"You want to fuck my ass?" Karen asked,"Uh, I would like that."

Rob pushed a little harder and soon he felt his cock entering her tight ass. God, this was good. She was so tight, but also very wet from the licking she had received before.

He started to fuck her harder and soon she was moaning with lust, it felt so good to be fucked in the ass.

Sharon was still busy with the younger boys cocks, they stood side by side and she stroked their cocks, only stopping when she sucked them. She even tried to have both their cocks in her mouth at the same time; it was a very hot sight to see her trying to fit them in her mouth.

Soon both boys were stroking their cocks themselves, Sharon was on her knees in front of them, waiting for them to shoot their cum all over her face.

"Chris, I'm going to cum," Peter moaned.

"Oh yeah, me too, let's give her our sperm," Chris replied.

Both boys were frantically jerking their cocks, trying to cum first. Peter thought it was just so cool having one of his friends joining him in having sex with his mom. Soon they could hold it no longer and the first spurt hit her on her forehead and soon both boys unloaded their cum on her face. The hot cum soon covered her cheeks and nose; she opened her mouth, trying to catch it as it spurts seemed to never stop. Both boys kept stroking their cocks, but eventually it ended and they used the cocks to smear it all over her face.

Rob looked at his mother getting a facial; it just looked so hot. He fucked Karen's ass even faster and he soon felt the familiar sensations in his groin.

"Oh fuck, I'm going to cum."

"Yes, cum in my ass, let me feel your hot cum in me."

He gave one final thrust and started to erupt in Karen's ass.

"Oh my god," Karen screamed, "I can feel you cum in my ass, it's so hot."

Rob kept fucking her, filling her ass with cum. At last he was done and he let his cock slip out of her ass.

He turned around and let his cum covered cock dangle before Sharon's eyes.

"Come on, clean my cock" he ordered.

She obediently opened her mouth and let the length of the glistering cock slide deep in her mouth. She licked and sucked his cock until he finally withdrew, stroking at a few times to make sure it was clean.

Karen got up and with hazed eyes she looked at Sharon.

"I need to be cleaned to," she said, while she approached Sharon.

She reached her mother-in-law and turned around and grabbed Sharon by the hair. She pushed her cum-covered face into her ass and moaned:

"Get your tongue to work. Lick my ass, lick your son's cum out of my ass."

The boys stared in awe at the sight before them. Sharon was licking excitedly at Karen's ass, moving her face up and down the crack. When her tongue slipped over her puckered hole, small squirts of white cum appeared, which she quickly lapped up.

When she was done, her face was covered with cum and her naked pussy was dripping.

Karen stood up and she was breathing hard. One hand caressed her tits and the other probed her pussy. She lifted one of her feet and let it touch Sharon's tits.

"You look like a real cum-slut, sperm all over you face. You want me to clean you?" she asked, while pushing Sharon to the floor.

Sharon's eyes widened, her answer came in gasps.

"If you have in mind what I think, yes, do it now"

Karen stepped a little closer, she was now standing over Sharon with one leg on each side of her big tits. She shuddered while she spread her pussy-lips.

"Are you ready, do you want to taste me?" she moaned.

"Oh yes, let me taste your juices"

Karen thrust her pussy a little forward and soon the first drops of her golden nectar fell from her, dripping on Sharon's tits.

The boys couldn't believe their eyes, was their mother actually asking Karen to pee on her. Their cocks were rock hard instantly and they stroked them without taking their eyes from the scenery in front of them.

The flow intensified and soon a steady stream of hot pee was hitting Sharon in the face. She opened her mouth and tasted the hot liquid. It was salty and had a slight rancid taste, but it was not unpleasant and she swallowed some.

"Oh yeah, drink my pee, you slut," Karen moaned, while she moved her pussy in circles, letting it rain all over Sharon.

When she was done, she quickly squatted over Sharon's mouth. She knew what she had to do and licked the waiting pussy clean.

Karen stood up and looked at the boys.

"Well, it sure looks as if you liked the show. If you're all ready, why don't let me help you cum all over her?"

All three boys quickly knelt in a semicircle around Sharon's face, while Karen was stroking their cocks. The show had been too much for them and after a little while, they started to erupt, Karen expertly directing the spurts of cum all over Sharon's face, which was soon covered in cum again. She swallowed most of it and rubbed the rest all over her tits.

A little while later Karen and the boys were sitting naked in the lounge, while Sharon was getting them something cold to drink.

"You know, Rob, I thought it was very cool to have Chris sharing our slut. Maybe we could invite others as well. What do you think?"

"Great idea. But why not let her be the prize for the team, if your no-good football team ever wins anything?"

Karen eyes lit up:

"Wow, that would be cool. Just imagine her with all the guys. I would love to see that."

At that moment Sharon came into the lounge, carrying a tray with cold beers and coke's.

"What would you love to, my dear?" she asked.

"Oh, you'll see. You might even like it" she giggled.

Later that night after Karen had left for work and Sharon had sucked them all off again, they sat in the kitchen, watching Sharon fill the dishwasher, her face still glistering with cum from the facials she just had received.

"Dad, Rob came up with an interesting idea today. You know my team hasn't won a game for as long as I can remember. If we brought mom along and promised the guys they could use afterwards, if we won, maybe that would do the trick.

"What a great idea. When is the next game?"

"It's already on Saturday. Do you really mean it, that would be great."

"You just go along as usual, I'll bring mom around for the pep-talk."

When they've gone to bed that night, Phil told her about the afternoon's conversation; she was shocked at the idea.

"Do you really want me to do all these dirty things outside the house? I'm not sure about that," she said.

"Sure, you'll be fine. They can keep their mouths shut; you know they are good boys."

"Well, I don't know. I mean, it's one thing Peter brings home a friend, but there are at least 15 guys in the team."

"Yeah, if they all turn up, that's about right. Just think of all the hard cocks and all the cum you can enjoy."

"Uh, yes. I'm getting all wet just thinking about that. Please fuck me now."

Phil quickly entered her and fucked her hard, all the time telling her how much she was going to enjoy being the center of attention.

They soon came and she went to sleep anticipating the weekend's action.

Peter came into the locker room and saw most of the players were already there. He was the team-leader and responsible for the tactics. He normally spent 15 minutes before the warm-up, explaining how he thought they should play.

This Saturday it was a little special, they played against their archrivals, which they had never beaten. So his surprise was perfect timing.

"Hi guys, listen. You all know whom we're playing against today. I want to win this game as much as you, but to inspire you a bit, I've arranged for a little reward, if we win."

He went to the door and opened it.

"Come on in, mom, meet the guys"

Sharon entered the locker room and some of the guys quickly grabbed their towels and covered themselves. She wore a long coat and when she was in the room, she locked the door behind her.

"Hi there. I just wanted to tell you, I'd be watching the game. If you play well and win the game, I'll be back to congratulate you."

When she said that, she dropped the coat and stood almost naked in the locker room. She wore high heels and stockings, crotch-less panties and a see-through bra, which only emphasized her big tits.

All the boys' just stared nobody said a word. They didn't believe their eyes, a naked woman in their locker room, a good-looking naked woman too.

Sharon grabbed her coat again and left the room. All hell broke loose after she left. They all wanted to know what she meant by what she said and Peter carefully explained, what it was all about.

They went out and played the game of their lives. They beat their rivals comfortably for the first time and were all shouting and screaming, when they came back to the locker room.

"Ok guys, well done. Now hit the showers, your reward are waiting."

They all scrambled to the showers and when they came back, Sharon was again standing in the room.

"Congratulations, you've played well. Now I want to see you all lined up."

The boys soon stood in one line and Sharon licked her lips at the sight. 15 nice young men, all very fit, with balls bursting with hot cum, just waiting for her. She felt a familiar sensation in her body, imagining the spurting cocks deliver their cum all over her body. She slowly walked down the line, looking at their cocks while she passed them. When she reached the end, she knelt and looked back. What a sight!

There were cocks in all sizes and colors. She was looking at a row of cocks, some fully erect, others hanging in a curve from the crotch.

She moved in front of the first three, taking a cock in each hand and sucking on the one in front of her. She took turns sucking all three cocks and when she was sure they were all fully erect and throbbing, she moved on to the next three. All the young men were eagerly stroking their cocks, she could see the hands moving up and down, while she was sucking on their friends.

When they were all ready, she was lifted up and carried to the showers, where she was placed on a bench. The first boy lifted her legs and entered her wet pussy in one thrust, and then started to fuck her. She took one cock in each hand and started to stroke them while another lowered his cock to her lips. She eagerly started to suck on it and was rewarded with a sudden gush of cum. The boy couldn't hold back and emptied the content of his balls in Sharon's mouth. He was soon done and withdrew his glistering member.

"Ok, who's next," Sharon called, her voice thick with cum, "I need more cock."

The next lined up and her mouth was soon again filled with cock. The guy fucking her came and she could feel the hot cum filling her pussy. When he stepped back, the next boy quickly took his place, thrusting his cock into her cum-filled pussy. She could hear the squishing sound it made as he fucked her. She felt the cocks in her hand begin to twist and she let go of the cock in her mouth.

"Come on, do it in my mouth, " she ordered the boys.

The moved up to her face and she opened her mouth, just in time to receive two huge loads of cum.. She could see they hadn't cum for days, it was thick and slowly dripping on her tongue. She kept in her mouth and when they were done, she let her tongue swirl it around in her mouth, playing with the sperm before she swallowed it.

They took turns fucking her like that for a while; her face and tits were now glistering with their juices. One guy placed himself on the floor and she was lifted from the bench and lowered onto the his cock. When she started to fuck the guy, she felt another pushing the head of his cock against her ass. She wriggled her ass and felt him slip in and soon he was fucking her hard and she enjoyed the feeling of being fucked in both holes at the same time.

When she looked up, she saw five guys standing before her, stroking their hard cocks. She licked her lips and said:

"Oh, that looks good, do you all have a nice load of cum for me? I want you all to cum in my face."

They came closer and she played with their swollen balls, while they were jerking off in her face. Soon she felt the hot cum hitting her face; she closed her eyes and let them plaster her face, the cum were dripping from her forehead and her nose when they were done.

Suddenly she felt a hard cock starting to feed the cum from her face into her mouth. She opened her eyes and saw the biggest cock she had ever seen. It was the black quarterback; he was standing in front of her cum covered face and stroked his cock.

She opened her mouth and let the ivory pole slip between her lips. It was so big, she could hardly wrap her lips around it, so she licked the head and let her tongue run along the underside down to his balls, which were enormous.

"Wow, you must have saved your cum for some days," said moaned.

"Yeah, the coach said no playing before the game, so I haven't cum for a week."

"Oh, then let me help you," Sharon said.

"Well, if you don't mind, Chris has told you also like to give rim-jobs. I never tried that:"

"Ok, turn around, but remember to tell me when you are ready to shoot your cum."

He quickly turned around and bent over. Sharon dragged the boy closer and let her tongue probe his ass. She slipped the tip over his puckered hole and licked up and down his crack, while she let her hands play with his big cock.

She could feel the boys fucking her drenched holes getting ready to cum and the cock between her hands started to twist.

"Quick, I'm coming," he shouted.

Sharon let go of his cock and he spun around, just in time to aim the first spurt in her face. She opened her mouth and spurt after spurt landed on her tongue, she couldn't believe how much cum he could hold. At the same time both guys fucking her filled her holes with hot cum and she came in a shuddering orgasm.

At last the orgy was over and she sat exhausted on a bench, her hair was drenched with cum and it ran from her pussy and ass down her legs. Phil came with a dress for her to wear on the way home and when she slipped it over her head, it immediately clung to her cum-soaked body.

"Well, how was that, you really seemed to like it."

"Yes, I have never seen and tasted so much cum in my life, it was wonderful."

"Ok, let's go home. There is a young lady waiting for you, she already had five beers to drink, she said she wanted to clean you up."

"You know what would be a great idea, we should invite the whole family to your next birthday. It's a long time since we had a real family party, would be great to see them again, don't you think" Phil asked.

"Mmm" Sharon answered, her mouth full of Phil's cock.

They were in their bedroom, they were watching a porn movie together and after having played with each other for a while, Phil have asked her to suck him off. She was naked, her big breasts pressing against Phil's stomach as she sucked his cock. She was also watching the movie where a blonde lady was on her knees, looking up at a circle of eight huge black cocks pointing at her face. Soon the guys started to cum and moved closer, the thick jets of cum landed on her upturned face.

"Hey, look at that, she getting so much cum, man that's so hot. Would you like to be in her place?"

"Oh yeah, that would be good to feel all the cocks spurting on my face, uhm I'm so horny, are you ready to cum?

On the screen the blonde had turned her face to the camera and her tongue was playing with the white sea of cum in her mouth while she was looking at the big cocks that were hanging half erect around her face.

That did it, Phil started to breathe faster and panted: " Oh yes, open your mouth"

Sharon stroked his hard cock faster and soon the cum splashed her face and shot into her mouth, it felt so good on her face, With the other hand she stroked her pussy and soon she came in a huge orgasm that shook her body.

After they had both cum, they lay embracing and talked about the party Phil had suggested.

"Are you sure that it will be ok to invite them all, I mean some of them might know what is going on in our house, but not all know and they might find out."

"Well, the way I have planned the party they will all know for sure. After all it is your birthday, so you should be the center of attention in more ways than being the hostess."

"What do you mean "in more ways than being the hostess" she asked?"

"The usual role of the hostess I'm sure you know, but for this party I would like to expand that role to be more intimate", Phil replied," but just let me handle the planning, I'll tell you what I mean later".

Next morning Phil told the rest of the family about the plans for a birthday party for the mom, they all thought it was a great idea.

Both Peter and Rob was exited to get to see all their relatives, both their cousins of which there were quite a few good-looking in between, but also some of their aunts whom they had been secretly admiring for years and who even now were very sexy.

Karen protested mildly:" Aren't there any well hung males in the family", she asked?

"Oh yes" Sharon said, " there are actually quite a number of good hunks in the family, don't you worry, you'll be in good company."

For the next few weeks they found time between their sexual escapades to organize the party and soon it was the night before the party. Phil had called them all into the kitchen and they sat around the table discussing tomorrow's party.

"Ok, I think we're all set for tomorrow, we just need to decide one last thing. What is your mother going to wear for the party?" Phil asked.

Sharon was sitting in her usual outfit, almost naked apart from black stocking and a garter belt.

"Well, I have this new white dress that I bought last year, I think that would be ok to wear", she said.

"I was actually thinking of a bit more revealing dress, since you are going to participate quite a lot in the entertainment as well", Phil said.

"What do you mean", the boys asked.

"Your mother is going to be a real family slut tomorrow, not just serving us, but all guest that needs entertaining. This is the part I have not told you about yet. Most of our family knows we're fucking each other and I know a lot of them do as well. So for the party tomorrow, you will be serving all the guests in whatever way they want."

"Oh boy, that sounds so hot," Peter said as he pulled out his cock and started stroking it.

"Can they do whatever they want?"

Karen grabbed Rob's cock and started jerking him off while she fingered herself. "If they want to have their cock sucked, they just tell her?"

"Yes, you will do whatever the guests want and wherever they like. So you will most likely find yourself on your knees or on your back most of the party, but I think that you will like it, you'll get lots of cock and get to taste some pussy, not to mention all the cum."

Sharon looked at Phil with big eyes.

"Do you really mean that? Don't you think some of the guests will be offended if we start to have sex during the party?"

"No, not at all, in fact I mentioned it in the invitation and all have come back and said they were looking forward to the party and the entertainment. Some of them even asked what they were allowed to do with you, I told them whatever they wanted to do was ok'"

Both boys and Karen were jerking off now, their minds racing thinking about the possibilities of having mind-blowing sex the next day.

"But I have bought some outfits you can try, we can then vote for the most sexy".

Phil fetched a bag with the dresses he had bought and soon Sharon found herself posing for the family in very revealing outfits. She could feel herself getting aroused, both because she actually liked parading like a model for her family, but also the thought of having sex with her relatives at the party tomorrow.

"So what do you think" she asked" I like the black most, but is it too much?"

She was wearing a black body stocking that let her big tits hanging exposed and only just covered parts of her ass, showing off her beautiful legs.

"I think it looks so sexy" Peter said, " If you come over here I'll show you what I mean".

She knelt down on the floor in front of him and he stroked his cock faster at the sight of his mother dressed like a true slut. Soon he started to moan and he pointed his cock at his mothers face.

"Oh my god, I can't wait to the party, here's a little taste of what to come" he gasped and soon his thick cum was spurting from his cock and hit Sharon's face, where it dripped from her nose and her chin. Soon Rob was ready as well and Karen dragged him by his cock in front of Sharon and jerked him off until he came. She pointed the spurting cock at her and let the cum cover her face, Sharon opened her mouth to catch it and Karen directed the last few spurts into her mouth.

"Mmmm, that was good" Sharon moaned.

Karen knelt down in front of her and started licking the cum off her face, it tasted so good and soon they were kissing, swapping the cum back and forth.

"Seems that you both are ready for tomorrow, it'll be a great party" Phil said.

The next day they were all exited and couldn't keep the hands off each other while they were waiting for the guests to arrive. Finally the first ones were there and they were greeted in the hall by the whole family. Sharon wore her black dress and Phil's brother and wife admired her sexy body, the brother fondling her big tits as he said hallo. Soon other started to arrive and Sharon was kissing and groping the guests, they in turn responded by grabbing her ass and fondling her tits, she was soon very wet and horny.

When they had all arrived, the family was making the rounds and getting all drinks.

"Hi everybody" Phil called, "Thank you all for coming to our little party. We're so glad to see you and especially Sharon has been looking forward to this. In a little while the dinner is ready, so please find your seats. Remember that we if you need something, we're all available for your every needs"

The table was set a one long table, made out of several glass-top tables put together. Soon all were seated, there were 24 people in all and some were noticing that there was no seat for Sharon. She stood at the end of the table and looked at her guests with lust in her eyes.

"Now that you're all seated, I hope you enjoy your dinner. As Phil mentioned in the invitation, I'll be the entertainment for tonight and I'll do my very best to fulfill all you requests. As you might know we have a very liberal attitude towards sex, so everything is allowed. I hope that you all have some dirty wishes, I'm really horny tonight."

After the starters were served, Phil's brother called for Sharon.

"Sharon, I've being dreaming about this party so long, I really need to get off"

She kissed him and without a word she crawled under the table and undid his pants. She reached inside and took out his half-hard cock and started to lick it. Soon he was sucking hard on his cock and the salvia was dripping from her mouth.

"Now that's entertainment" Sharon's sister said.

All could see Sharon sucking off Phil's brother, some were a little shocked, but most were enjoying the sight. Sharon's sister was rubbing her husband's hard cock through his pants, his eyes were fixed on Sharon's mouth gliding up and down the hard cock. Soon Phil's brother started to squirm in the seat and Sharon sucked harder.

"Do you think she will swallow his cum" Sharon's sister asked.

"Oh yes, she absolutely loves cum. Normally she'll suck all of us off at least once a day and she always swallows if we don't cum on her face" Peter said.

"Well, she in for a treat, I have tried for a week to make him cum, but she have saved it all for today" Phil's sister-in-law said while she was rubbing her pussy.

Phil's brother started panting hard, Sharon took his cock deep into her mouth and he with a groan he started to cum in her mouth. All could see that Sharon's mouth quickly filled with cum, her cheeks bellowed and cum started to flow from the sides of her mouth, running down the cock still filling her mouth. She swallowed hard and after a few more jerks, she opened her mouth and let the cock pop out and started to lick the cum of it. She had a dreamy look in her eyes as she held the glistening cock in her hand, licking it and slurping the juices of it. They could all see the cum in her mouth and on her tongue.

When she was done, all clapped and she looked up though the table and grinned at the guests.

"Oh wow, thanks for the present, that was some load, so much and so tasty. I hope that there are more presents like this" she said with a smile.

A little further down the table Karen was chatting with Peter's cousin, she nodded several times and then called for Sharon. She came up to Karen and stood beside her, then bend over and kissed her.

"Umh, I see what you mean, that cum tastes so good. Listen, Brian here is too shy to ask, but he got so horny seeing you suck cock, would you do that to him as well?"

"I would love to, I hope that he's got a lot of cum for me"

Sharon knelt in front of him, Karen had already taken Brian's cock out. The tip was wet with his pre-cum and Sharon licked it off, using the tip of her tongue to play with it. She took the cock in her hand and started to jerk him off. Some of the guests were openly rubbing their pussies, some had their cocks jerked off by the women and all were watching Sharon. But the poor guy was so excited that before Sharon could take it in her mouth, he came in big spurts all over her face. The first strands covered her nose and chin, she quickly opened her mouth and caught the rest in her mouth. The spurts subsided and she took the cock in her mouth and licked it clean.

When she got up, she stood for a moment and looked at the guests, cum dripping from her face unto her big tits. They all applauded again and she licked her lips.

"Anyone else needs service" she asked

Almost everyone raised their hands, she smiled and crawled back under the table. When she looked down the row of people on both sides of her, she could see hard cocks and fingers busy between legs. She started to lick the first pussy, it tasted so good and soon the juices were flowing, she could see the hard cocks next to her being jerked off, this was heaven.

When the lady being licked had cum, Sharon got out from under the table and told the guest that she now needed to be fucked. She went to the living room where a bed has been prepared, laid on her back and spread her legs, rubbing her dripping pussy.

"Who wants to be first, I need a hard cock" she said smiling

One of Phil's brothers quickly jumped on the bed and stuck his hard cock into her wet pussy, fucking her hard while she gasped. She quickly reached an orgasm but he continued to fuck her hard. Around them some were watching, fingers in pussy or on a hard cock, others were fucking. Karen handled three cocks at once, Rob was in her pussy and another fucking her ass while a third was being sucked off.

"Oh, fuck me, fuck me hard" Sharon screamed, nearing another good cum.

Phil's brother couldn't hold back anymore and with a groan he started to unload his cum in her pussy, Sharon moaned as she felt the hot cum filling her up and soon she came , adding her own juices to his cum.

He slowly withdrew and left her pussy wide open, dripping with cum and cuntjuice. Sharon was still panting hard, her eyes filled with lust as she felt the wetness of her cunt with her hand. One of her nephews entered the bed, stroking his hard cock, Sharon spread her cuntlips and he entered her wet pussy, not minding the fact that it was filled with cum, he could feel it oozing out of her pussy as he thrust his cock up her pussy.

"Oh my god, I'm so wet, make me cum again you horny bastard"

Sharon's sister was approaching the bed, dragging her youngest son with her, he was still fully clothed, but his eyes were filled with excitement of watching so many of his family members fucking and sucking, you could see the outline of his cock at the front of his pants.

"Sharon, Joe here would also like to give you a present but since you're occupied I'll unwrap it for you" she said smiling.

She placed her son at the end of the bed and started to undo his pants, Sharon looked mesmerized as she pulled out the largest cock she had seen for a long time.

"Well thank you Joe, just what I wanted. Come here, let me suck on it."

Joe knelt on the bed beside her head and she took the almost hard cock in her hand, lifting it slowly over face, marveling at its size. It was at least 10 inches long and very thick, slowly getting harder and throbbing in her hand.

"Mmm sis, he has such a wonderful cock, do you get to enjoy it as well?"

"Oh yes, Joe regular fucks me, I love to feel his thickness in my pussy. Especially in the morning before he goes to work, but a nice evening fuck after Ben has had his turn is also good. He is still young and he has so much cum, try to feel his balls" Sharon's sister said.

Sharon felt her nephew's balls, they were big and hard and she was looking forward to a big load.

"Come closer, let me see if it fits in my mouth. I want all your cum in my mouth, would you like that?" she teased the young man.

"Oh yes, just like my mother likes, she also loves when I empty myself in her mouth. But watch out, I cum a lot"

Sharon opened her mouth and sucked at the head, opened up as much as she could and started to let the hard cock slide into her mouth. She could only manage to fit half of the length in her mouth, so she used her hand to jerk him off while she was sucking him.

Karen had another orgasm, she was still being serviced by the three guys, but they were fucking her faster now, getting closer to cum. Karen was so horny, having two cocks in her holes and one to suck on was the best she ever had tried. She could also see Sharon getting fucked and at the same time sucking on a huge cock, she looked as she was in heaven as well.

Around the room most of the guests were sucking and fucking, Phil was pounding his hard cock into his niece's wet pussy, her big tits bouncing with his trust. Peter was licking the wet cunt of his aunt, he had secretly admired her mature body for years, getting a hardon when looking at her shapely legs, sexy feet and her big tits. Now she was naked in all her glory and laying on her back, Peter's head buried between her legs where he was licking her wet pussy and sometimes letting the tongue slip further down and probing her delicious ass. She had cum several times and was now begging for him to fuck her. He got up and kissed her, she could taste her own juices on his lips.

"Peter, let me feel you hard cock in me, don't let me wait any longer. I have waited to be fucked by you for years, I could see you always was horny when you visited"

Peter was happy to obey, he started to fuck her wet pussy, his big cock pounding away in the slippery wetness. After a while, he let it slide out and pressed it against her puckered hole, looked up at her when he saw she was smiling and nodding, he started to let it slide slowly into her ass, enjoying the feeling of the tightness of her ass.

"Oh yes, fuck me in the ass, let me feel your big cock in there" she panted

At the same time Sharon was sucking and jerking Joe's big cock, massaging the shaft while she was sucking, soon she felt it begin to throb and she let it out of her mouth, playing with it and looking up at Joe with a dirty grin.

"Are you ready to cum? I can feel you getting there" she smiled

"Oh yeah, I want to cum in your mouth so bad" he said, at the same time playing with her big tits.

Her other nephew heard Sharon begging for it, he soon started to cum in her pussy. Joe was breathing harder now, looking at the horny lady jerking his cock, her pussy overflowing with cum and her mouth open, ready to accept his sperm.

"Oh god, I'm almost there, oh yes" he groaned

Most of the guests were watching the action on the bed, Sharon lying there with cum oozing out from her used pussy, her hand slowly playing with Joe's cock. She was teasing him, drawing out the orgasm, but at last she gripped the cock harder and jerked faster.

"Arrgh, I'm cumming" he panted

The guests and Sharon watched in fascination as the huge cock twisted and released huge spurts of cum, the first hit Sharon straight in the face, then she quickly directed the rest towards her mouth. The cum kept spraying from the cock and her mouth was soon almost overflowing. At last he was done and he fell on the bed, completely exhausted.

Sharon was still on her back, mouth open with dreamy eyes, the tongue playing with the cum Joe had unloaded in her mouth. Her sister knelt on the bed next to her.

"Uhh, that looks so hot. I told you he would cum a lot, but I think he might have skipped a session or two. Let me taste it"

She bent down and let her tongue slip into Sharon's mouth, dipping it in the cum and licking Sharon's lips. They started to kiss harder, sharing the cum, the others could see it dripping from the corners of their mouths.

"Oh my god, that is so hot" Rob groaned

He started to fill Karen's pussy with cum and soon the other two also unloaded in her ass and on her face. Karen screamed as she came, the sensation of being filled in both end at the same time pushed her over the edge.

On the bed Sharon's sister had moved to the end of the bed and was now licking her wet pussy, enjoying the mixed juices from Sharon and the men that fucked her. Karen got up and went to the bed, cum dripping from her face.

"Well. It looks like you have gotten what you wanted, are you up for more"

"Yes, that was a very good and tasty load, but I still want more" Sharon said, enjoying her sisters tongue between her legs.

THE END

Share your thoughts with us.
Take a moment to tell us how we're doing. Your feedback really matters.

You can reach us by:
Email: my777books@yahoo.com

Search for other titles by Sophie MacDonald.

www.ingramcontent.com/pod-product-compliance
Lightning Source LLC
LaVergne TN
LVHW011255200326
834410LV00006B/272